Baby Grady
The First Year

Author: Laura Holmes
Illustrator: Walter Schmidt

PublishAmerica
Baltimore

First printing

ISBN: 1-4137-3202-X
PUBLISHED BY PUBLISHAMERICA, LLLP
www.publishamerica.com
Baltimore

Printed in the United States of America

Dedication:

For Greg—Thanks for everything.
For all dogs—Thanks for the laughs.

Acknowledgements

I would like to thank my first audience: Greg, Rich and Judy, Paul and Jessica—thanks for your encouragement.

Special thanks to my first readers: Mom and Susan.

And a big thank you to Walter and Kathryn, the story wouldn't be the same without you!

And thanks to everyone else that listened to the idea of the story and offered their words of support. I really appreciate it.

Introduction

My name is Grady. AKA Baby Grady, Grades, the Gradester, or the Grademeister. People have called me a lot of names over the years, but for some reason Baby Grady seemed to stick. Strangers and friends alike call me Baby Grady. People are always stopping me on the street and saying nice things to me. And I'm nice to them. Now. But it wasn't always that way.

One of my earliest memories was in my first home. I had friends and brothers and a sister, and we would play all day long. I was still pretty young when two people came by to adopt one of us. That means that one of us would leave here and go home to live with them. Even though I was young, I knew how it worked.

There was a man—tall and serious looking. He was dressed nicer and smelled better than most of the men I knew so I thought that maybe he was important. Like maybe he owned a factory or something. And I got even more excited when I let my imagination run wild and thought that it might be a food factory. Wouldn't that be the best? Going home with someone that owns a food factory!!

And the lady seemed just as nice. She was smaller than the guy and she laughed a lot. When the other boys and I would get all around her and make noise, she seemed a little nervous and would jump if one of us got rough. But then she would laugh and pat the top of someone's head. And she kept smiling. We were certainly trying to be noticed that day, and I think she noticed each one of us.

They seemed serious that day about finding an addition to their family, and the owners were more than eager to put us on show and remind us to be on our good behavior. Some of the older boys couldn't help but act silly and vie for attention, but my friends and I thought: If they want us, they'll pick us, and we're not going to act all silly and prance around like no one loves us. We have each other and that's all we need. That's all we'll ever need.

But then we looked closer. These people seemed really nice. I knew that I wanted them to pick me. I just knew it. But I didn't know how to prance and strut my stuff like the older boys. So I panicked. I ran around in circles and made more noise than any of the others. I ran over to the lady as she was bending down to talk to my friend, and I just put my head in her lap. All I kept thinking was: Please pick me, please pick me, please pick me.

I must have started some kind of ruckus, because before I knew it, there were a lot of my friends doing the same thing. I knew now that I could never compete. I just wanted them to choose me so badly that I lost it. But, as you'll see once you get to know me, I'm not one to give up. So I thought I'd try again. I pushed my friends aside and just grabbed at the lady's leg. And do you know what? She started to laugh. She said, "I like this little boy. He certainly is persistent. What do you say? Can we get him? Check with the people. Make sure he's available. I'd love to take this one home."

And then she sat with me and talked to me and told me how lucky they would be if they could have me come to live with them. If they only knew who the lucky one would be!

Then I found out that they did pick me! And I was going home with them!

The three of us got into the car and that's when I realized I would be leaving my friends. I looked out the window while the lady held me and I smiled, not a bragging smile, 'cause I knew how it felt to be left behind. But a kind of "be happy for me" smile. And they smiled back. I knew they were happy for me. Real friends are happy when you do well. If they aren't happy when you're happy, then they aren't your real friends. How could they not be happy for me? Right then I was the luckiest boy in the world.

So that's how I ended up at this house, living with Greg and Laura. Remember, I'm only recalling memories now, and looking back on them always makes me smile.

My New Name

I am in the front seat, riding on the floor between the lady's legs. But mostly she picks me up and talks "baby talk" to me. "What a cutie, cutie, cutie, you are" and "you are sooooo cute." This goes on for a while and I am liking it. Someone is paying attention to me. All I have to do is smile and lick her and she keeps saying nice things. And she keeps patting my head and rubbing around my ears. Everyone knows that's the best. Then she calls me her "cute little Baby Grady." And that's when I realize that I really like that new name. (My old name was Spotty because of the white spot on my chest.) These people are going to call me Baby Grady. And man, I like it! Yeah, that is my new name and I like it!

But the name causes a little bit of a problem between the lady and the guy. She keeps calling me Baby Grady and he keeps saying, "Grady, just Grady." At this point I don't care what they call me—Grady, Baby Grady, or Just Grady.

But he says, "I don't know any 150 pound guy that wants to be called baby anything."

And the lady says, "He's not 150 pounds yet, he's just a baby. And besides, I think he likes it."

Then he says, "You know we agreed on Grady. I think we should call him Grady. Just Grady."

That's when she responds with, "Ok, you can call him Grady. And I'll call him Grady. But sometimes I might call him Baby Grady, 'cause he's just such a cute little Baby Grady. And I think he likes it."

She is right about that. I do like Baby Grady. But on this particular day, with these two people, they could call me Grady, Baby Grady, Just Grady, or any kind of Grady. All I know is that I am Grady, and I am going home with these great people.

My New Big Brother

Wow! What a big dog! Is it my cousin, my uncle, or better yet, my new brother? Who is this big guy? I knew I liked these people, but bringing me here to this big dog is the best! I think I love this dog. Let me sniff him some more just to be sure. I've heard about boys that are too trusting. Not me, I'm going to be careful around this guy. I'm always going to be careful. Okay, he seems okay. Kinda mellow and not saying much and all. Maybe he hasn't seen a little guy like me in a while. Maybe he's never seen such a cute little fellow like me before—ever. I'll give him a chance to sniff me. Once he gets to know me, he'll love me. I know this lady sure loves me already. What a fuss she makes!

Hey, wait a minute. Just you wait one minute. Now she's making a fuss over the big guy too. Does she know him? Hey, she's kissing him on the nose and head too! I thought I was the one she kissed like that. Who is this big guy, anyway? Would someone just tell me that?

Just then, the guy makes some kind of introductions. But I'm not as happy as I was about five minutes ago, so I'm not paying as much attention. But the fact is that this is my brother Moose. (Isn't that a strange name? You have to admit that it's not nearly as cute as Baby Grady.) And since the lady seems to like Moose a lot, and he *is* my big brother, and he hasn't bothered me too much yet, I think I'll go back to liking him too. Remember, five minutes ago I had nearly fallen in love with him and I didn't even know who he was then. Now that I know he's my big brother, well, I'll give him a chance.

Now we're walking into the house together. The nice lady, the nice guy, my big brother Moose, and me. And me. I'm going into a house with my family. My very own family.

Taking Care of Business

When we get into the house I am amazed. There is a big fancy room with couches and tables and other things (remember, I just came from the breeder's barn). Then there are other rooms with other tables and other things that I have no idea what they are. And then, after they let me sniff everything, under their close watch, they take me up higher in the house, up some stairs. And up there is even more stuff. Rooms with beds and furniture and a room with just a desk and books.

And there is a room that is a little cooler than the others. There is a big drinking bowl that makes noise when you press down on a handle. And it gets new water for you then. And a big huge tub of some kind that gets water in it too. But I don't know what that's used for yet.

At this point I still can't believe my luck. This place is huge! And it smells so nice. I guess my brother Moose does his "business" somewhere else. 'Cause he's a big guy and I don't think it would smell so nice in here if he could go wherever he wanted. I'll have to find out about the arrangements later. Right now I'm just happy to be here and trying to get to know the place.

The lady and the guy are right with me the whole time. They

must want to be around me all of the time. They won't let me explore on my own at all. But that's okay. I like being around them. They talk to each other and laugh. They keep saying things like "remember, stay with him, we don't want him doing what Shadow did to the house."

I don't know what Shadow is, but I know I won't do what the Shadow did to the house. I'm going to try my hardest to be the best little boy for these people. And for Moose. He's been following us around for a while, but he doesn't go into every room with us. I guess he already knows the house. But it's all new to me, and I'm just loving it. I guess it shows, because I can't stop sniffing and wagging, and wagging and sniffing.

And then the lady picks me up and says, "I can't believe I can pick him up! It's so nice to have a little one to pick up. I don't remember the last time I could pick up Shadow. All I remember is that one day she was pretty little, and then one day I couldn't pick her up anymore. Remember, Greg?"

Aha!! The guy's name is Greg. Now I have something to call him. His name is Greg. I like that name too. It even kinda matches with Grady. Grady and Greg. Greg and Grady. Yeah, I like these names. I just have to find out the lady's name. I think it would be nice if it began with a G too. Like Gregie. Yeah, Gregie, Greg and Grady. You have to admit, it sounds like a family. I know there's Moose too, but he's been here awhile and doesn't need to sound like he fits in.

And, to tell you the truth, I don't know any other lady names that begin with a G, even to imagine one. I am just a baby you know. So I'll just have to wait and see what Greg (I love knowing his name!) calls her.

Back to the house tour. Greg and the lady show me all of the rooms in the house. Moose is interested at first but either can't keep up—remember, he is pretty big—or loses interest. I'll have to ask him later. So far he hasn't said much of anything to me. Maybe he doesn't talk much when the lady and Greg are around. Maybe he still doesn't understand who I am or what I am doing here. Well, I hope that Greg and the lady told him I was coming here to live and he doesn't think I'm just an afternoon visitor. Someone that just says a polite hello and then leaves. I sure hope that's not what he's thinking. 'Cause if there's one thing I know, it's that I'm not leaving here. Ever.

Oh, if you thought the house was wonderful, let me describe the outside! There is a brick patio with a table on it. And by the way, I know that tables are bought so that little guys have something to climb on and walk around on and be higher than others. And so far in the house I counted four tables. Plus this one. Yeah, I'll be getting my exercise. But besides the cool bricks and table, there is so much room to run. But there is a fence so you can't run too far. I think Greg and the lady think like I do. You never can be too careful. Don't want a little guy like me running into the street or meeting tangled-haired street characters. No sir. Fences are okay by me.

When we go outside Moose is lying on the patio as if he's done it all of his life. Oh yeah, he might have done it all of his life. I keep forgetting that he knew these people for I don't know how long before I came along today. Well, maybe he has been on the patio every day for a lot of years, that doesn't mean that we can't share. Isn't that what brothers do? Share?

I'm sure that we'll both be hanging out on this patio in no time.

But when I look at Moose, I don't think he's so keen on me hanging out with him. He's not saying anything in front of Greg and the lady, but he's not so friendly out here on the patio. His patio. Yep, he pretty much just told me under his breath that it was his patio.

Well, that's okay. Who wants to stay outside on a patio anyway when there is a huge house with lots of tables and things to occupy your time? And it is rather cold out here. It was cold at the breeder's too. I'm kinda used to the cold, and the guys at the breeder said we were the kind of dogs that were supposed to like the cold. Well, I like it and all, but if my new brother Moose likes to be out here by himself, I'll let him. I think it's nicer in the house anyway. And warmer. And I'm getting the feeling that the lady doesn't like the cold so much. So maybe she spends her time inside. And if she spends her time inside, that's where I'll be spending my time. With her. In the house. So, brother Moose, as much as I would like to hang with you on "your" patio, I think I'll stay inside with the lady.

Oh, wait. Greg's not letting me inside yet. After about only ten minutes the lady says she's cold so she goes inside. But Greg keeps telling me to "pee." I hear what he's saying and I sure do want to do whatever he's asking me to do, but I don't understand him. "Grady, we can go in as soon as you pee. Just pee, Grady, then we can all go inside. I'm getting cold, Grady, but you have to start peeing out here. The sooner the better. Just pee, Grady."

Well, I certainly would pee if I knew what pee meant. But

I don't. So I walk around, watching Greg's face to see if I'm doing what he wants me to do. I start moving some stones with my nose on the side of the shed. Nope, that's not peeing. I really didn't think it was, but hey, no loss in trying. So I keep walking around. I pull out some ivy from the fence with my teeth. Maybe that is peeing. Nope, another strike. I keep watching Greg's face to see his reaction, to see if I did his pee, even if by accident. But no such luck.

He waits and keeps saying, "C'mon Grady, Buddy, Gradester, let's just go pee, then we can go in." As much as I want to be his buddy and do what he wants me to do, I can't. Because I don't know what pee means.

Then Moose steps in. He's been listening and watching the whole time on the patio. I didn't pay that much attention to him because I was just looking and watching Greg's face to see if I gave him what he wanted. You can always tell if you give someone what they want by their face. They smile and look at you with the "nice eyes." You now, the kind of eyes that seem to smile too. And then sometimes they say the nice things too—to let you know that you did what they wanted. And that's why I was looking so closely at Greg's face and I didn't pay that much attention to Moose.

But I think I should have been paying attention to Moose too. I think he could help me to know what pee means more than Greg. So now, I look at Moose and it seems like he's smiling and has those smiling eyes like people, when he looks at me and says, in the deepest, calmest, nicest voice I ever heard, "Just find somewhere on that side of the yard," and he motions to the left, "and squat and leak. You know, squat and leak like you always do when you gotta let it go. "Pee" just means "take a leak," "let it go," "number one," "tinkle," "tee tee," "drain the vein," "hose the yard." I know you have to know some of those phrases. "Pee" is just these people's way of saying all of those other kennel terms. Even a baby like you has to know what ONE of those things mean."

"Well, why didn't you tell me sooner? Of course I know what THOSE words mean. I might be a baby, Baby Grady, but I wasn't born yesterday. You don't know anything about my past. I certainly do know what Greg wants now.

"And by the way, thank you. I mean it. I could have been out here all day and not known what he wanted. And you could have been mean and laughed at me and wanted Greg not to like me and think I was stupid or something. So thanks, Moose. I'll try to make it up to you someday."

"Don't worry about it. Even though I don't want to share my patio with you, I'm not mean. You were right about one thing. I don't know anything about where you came from or what you did before today. But just remember, you don't know anything about my past before I came here to Laura and Greg's house, or anything about the past five years I've been alone with them."

I understand what he is saying, and I will try hard to remember that he was here first, but he said something way too exciting to think of anything else.

The lady's name is Laura. Not Gregie, or any other G name. Laura. Laura, Laura, Laura. Greg, Laura, Grady and Moose. I think I'm going to like it here even more than I ever dreamed.

The Cage

I can't believe they want me to sleep in a CAGE all during the night! I never, ever slept in a cage before. My old owners would put down fresh straw and make sure everyone was okay. Even the bad boys didn't have to sleep in CAGES. And they keep telling me what a good boy I am and how cute I am, and how much they love me. A CAGE?

The set-up is that Greg and Moose sleep upstairs where there is a bed and Laura and I sleep in the room with the couches. There is a short table and other tables, but they have them pushed to the side so that the CAGE fits. It's only my first night here, and I think I'm a trooper, you know, willing to try all kinds of things, but a CAGE? I just keep thinking that if Greg and Laura (I still just love saying their names) love me so much, why the CAGE? I don't remember seeing a cage upstairs by the bed for Moose. So if he doesn't have to sleep in a cage, why do I? And no one will tell me why.

So I cry. I don't want to cry. But I have to. Right now I miss the smell of straw and my old buddies. And snuggling close to everyone. Not to mention Mother. How I miss hearing her breathe and cuddling with her as close as

I could get. So I keep crying. I know I thought I was ready to leave, heck, I was even excited to leave. But right now, in the dark, in a strange room, with a lady I just met, in a CAGE, I can't help but to cry. And cry.

Laura is sleeping right outside the CAGE. She even puts her hand on mine and tells me that everything is going to be okay. And she says it in such a nice, soft, kind of sing-song voice. "It's okay, Baby Grady. I know you're just a baby, but it'll be okay. You'll see. We already love you sooooo much. You're going to love it here. I'll play with you and Greg can't wait to take you for a walk in the snow. And you'll love Moose. He's such a nice boy. And he really wanted to have a baby brother. We told him all about you before you came. And he told me that he couldn't wait for you to come. You'll see. Everyone loves you. And you haven't even met a lot of people that will love you. It's okay, baby. My little, tiny, Baby Grady."

Her words sound nice. And I know she means everything. And I want to stop crying, even if it is just to make her feel better. But I still feel sad, and I can't help it. And I can't stop crying. And she can't stop telling me nice things to make me feel better.

Somehow we both manage to fall asleep. But when I get hungry, I wake up and started crying and barking for my food. That's what I always did, what all of the boys did. I remember what a noise we would make and the commotion we would cause at the breeder's like it was yesterday. Oh yeah, it was only yesterday. Well, anyway, I'm hungry and I don't know how this food thing works around here, but I want someone to know I'm hungry.

Then I have another recollection from yesterday. I remember I thought that Greg might own a dog food factory. He does seem important. And he has this nice house and all. But then, even if he owns a dog food factory, it's not right here. I know that much. Because I would surely smell the food by now. And I'm not smelling food. I'm not smelling any of the smells I'm used to in the morning. Oh, where is my food? Where is my food?

I don't have to worry so much after all. As soon as I start to bark a little and cry a little, Laura is awake and flying into action. She lets me out of my CAGE, puts on her coat and opens the back door. The cold air catches us both off guard, but I can't wait to get out. The ground is frozen hard and I can see my breath. But over to one side of the yard it isn't all frozen and there is a little mud. Oh, I am going to like this yard. I'm liking it now. I run around like I own the place. Well, in a way I do own the place. I mean, I live here and all. And when Moose isn't in the yard, I'm king of the yard. King of the wet, cold earth. That's me. King Grady.

But then Laura interrupts my fantasies with, "Baby Grady, you have to pee before you can eat. C'mon baby, just pee so you can go in and eat."

Well, now I really owe Moose one. I would never want Laura to think I'm stupid, so I'm so glad I found out what pee means. I walk over to the left side of the yard and "let it go. "Then she claps for me and tells me what a good boy I am and we walk back into the house. Once inside, she starts to fix my breakfast. I have no idea what it's going to be, so I have to watch her every move. You never can be too careful—especially where food is concerned.

Hey, someone must have told her what I like! She's making my favorite breakfast. Even if Greg doesn't own a food factory I know I'll be okay now. And she's being real careful, giving me my pills and all. Yeah, this early morning routine with Laura might be okay. Back yard, food,—like I said, I'm going to like it here.

But now she wants me to do something else. I just ate, and it was excellent, so all I really want to do is go back to sleep. Not in the CAGE, but I'm going to try and get around that. But she wants me to go back outside. Okay, a little early to actually start my day, but I'm a trooper. Now she's telling me to "poop." And she's being so nice about it, I think I should poop for her, but I don't know what it means. And Moose isn't here to tell me. Oh, no. After only one day, I'm depending on my brother. I was determined to have him think that I was pretty worldly and didn't need his help. But now I need it again. If I only knew what "poop" means.

Uh-oh. I feel the very sudden urge to "poo poo," as the breeders would say. I don't know where to go. I know! I'll go over to the left where Moose told me to pee and do it there. Okay, now I feel much better. And Laura's clapping and telling me what a good boy I am. Now why would she clap when I "poo poo"? Very odd. All of the boys "poo poo" and it's no big deal. But she thinks it is, and now she wants to go inside.

I get it! "Poop" is the same as "poo poo," and I just did it! I did it for Laura. Just like she asked. And without Moose's help. Not to underplay how much he helped me yesterday with the pee thing, but maybe he still can think I'm not such a baby after all.

Mud, Mud, Mud

Every day is so much fun. Laura and I get up early and play outside. Well, I play and she pleads. "Please just pee and poop, Baby Grady. Please, I'm cold and tired—we can play later—it's so early!" She says just about the same thing every day. But I can't just do my business and go inside. I just can't. This is the only time of the day that Moose isn't out here, the air is nice and fresh, and there is just so much to do! And when it rains, oh, the mud. I think that mud is the best thing in the world. Every time I come outside I try to find some mud. Mud, mud, mud. I like the sound of it, the feel of it, the smell of it, the taste of it, and just the sight of it can send me into a dive. I dive for it every chance I get. I roll in it and try to get as much on my face as possible. Oh, I love mud all right.

But Laura and Greg don't share my feelings for mud. I've never seen either one of them ever play in it. And they try to keep me away from it. And when I get into it, they take it off of me as soon as they can. Now I know what that big tub upstairs is used for—taking the mud off of me.

But I've seen Laura and Greg use it too and they don't even play in mud. So I don't know why they use it. But every time they catch me with mud all over my body, they pick me up and take me upstairs and wash it off. Sometimes they even hose me off outside first, then take me up to the tub. They don't seem happy, especially Laura, but then I get to play in the water in the tub. I pretend like I don't like it, you know, by trying to get out of the tub and even looking sad. Laura always falls for the sad look. So even if she is mad about the mud, when she sees my droopy-eyed, head-lowered sad look, she gets sweet talking again.

"It's okay, Grady. I know you're just a baby. But we don't like it when you get all muddy. It makes everything so dirty. You get dirty, the kitchen floor gets dirty, the carpeting gets dirty, the tub, the towels, everything. You have to stop rolling in the mud every time we let you out. Understand?"

Well, I know everything gets dirty—that's why mud is so great! Dirty feels good. And if I feel good when I'm dirty, the things I get dirty probably feel good too. So I'm really doing everyone a favor, see?

But I know she doesn't see it my way. Because every time I get into the mud, she gets mad and I get a bath. I don't think she knows that I like the mud *and* the bath. Sometimes the bath is the only reason I play in the mud. So I can spend time alone with Laura. She has really nice fingernails that she runs up and down my back when the shampoo is on. And after my sad look, she always goes back to talking nice to me. So the mud and the bath are two of my favorite things right now.

The Training

Another thing that I like right now is the "training". Every day Laura takes me out and we have lessons. Usually we work on SIT, STAY, and COME. All I have to do now is watch Laura's face to see if I'm doing what she wants. And each time I do what she wants, I get a kibble. Kibble is just another word for a treat. So all morning, or however long training lasts, I get treats. But I have to do it right to get the treat. And the STAY is really hard to do. Especially since I know that kibble is waiting.

Moose lies on the patio and watches the training. I think he gets a kick out of watching me have a hard time with the STAY, because that's the one he watches the most. Besides the fact that he enjoys watching me, I know he's out there for another reason. Sometimes, even though he's not the one doing all of the work, Laura gives him a kibble anyway. All he does is lie there and watch, smile when I goof, and he gets a treat! Go figure.

So when Laura's taking a break, I ask Moose why he doesn't have to be "trained."

He says, in that deep throated voice of his, "Laura and Greg got me when I was already over a year old. My old owners never spent the time training me. So I wasn't very nice to them. Not that I didn't want to be nice, but I didn't know how to be. And they weren't very nice to me. Not very nice at all. They did things to me that no little guy like yourself should even know about. But enough about that.

"When Laura and Greg found me, I didn't know how to do anything either, even though I was already a big guy. Everyone thought that I should know how to SIT, STAY, and COME because I was so big. But I didn't. So Greg took me to a class where there were other dogs that were all going to learn the commands. But they were all puppies, and I was a dog. I was so big compared to all the others, even Laura laughed. I know she didn't mean to hurt my feelings, but she did. She said, 'Oh Greg, he looks like Jethro in the 6th grade. I can't even look, he looks so funny. And sad, like he knows he looks funny. Let's not make him do this anymore. We'll train him at home. Please. Let's get him out of here.'

"That was one of the nicest things they ever did for me. And I'll never forget it. Anyway, they did try to train me at home. But since I was older, it didn't take long. The key is to watch their faces as closely as possible. The face will even let you know if you are getting close to doing what they want. That's the best advice I can give you. Watch the face, and do what you think they want. And, Grady, it does get easier. Every time you practice, it'll get easier. That's why she does it with you every day, so it'll get easier. You'll learn soon enough, the more you practice, the happier she'll get. And then they will always treat you really well, trust me on that.

"And if you ever get tired of the training, just remember that they are doing it so that you'll be safe. The fact that they spend time training you means that they really care about you.

Consider yourself lucky. My old owners didn't care enough to spend the time training me."

That was the most Moose has said to me yet. And what good advice! Watch the face, he said. Okay, I'll watch the face. I kinda was already doing that. Remember, I wasn't born yesterday, I know when to watch a face.

The training means that they love me. Moose said "care about," but I know he means "love." Okay, then I guess it's a good thing that she is training me.

And he told me a little bit about his life before this house. It sounded like he didn't have it easy. Imagine, owners that don't like you. I really can't imagine. Moose is a good looking guy. And he's nice too. But maybe he wasn't as cute as I am when he was a pup—and he already said he didn't know how to be nice. Imagine having to be taught how to be nice. I guess it just comes naturally to me. So all that this training can really do is to teach me to be nicer. Yeah, I'll be nicer. Nicer than Moose—and he seems nicer to me all the time. Maybe I'll be the nicest dog in the world. Yeah, king of the nice. People will come from miles around to see the nicest dog in the world. And Laura and Greg will be so proud. And so happy that they picked me. And I'll be the very best SITTER, COMER, and STAYER the world has ever seen!

Laura interrupts my imagination again. Time for more training. Watch the face. I have to remember that.

Left Alone

It seems as though Laura and Greg don't spend all of their time in the house with us. After only a few days I realize that they leave sometimes. I have no idea where they go, 'cause if I did, I would just follow them. But they go in the car. I know that much. And sometimes they are gone for what seems like forever. I don't know how to tell time, but if I did, I would still know that they go away for a long, long time. And it seems even longer because it's usually dark. (And I hate to admit it, but I don't like the dark. Mainly because you can't see the things that are there that might hurt you. You never can be too careful.)

At least I have Moose here. But he isn't always near me because he's not in a CAGE and I am. I don't see why I have to be the one in the CAGE. If I were allowed to run free I know I'd be good. I'd just hang with Moose and shoot the breeze. We could be like real brothers, swapping stories and having fun. But no, I'm in a CAGE in the living room and Moose is wherever he pleases. It's just not fair.

But sometimes Moose comes and sits by my CAGE. I think he knows that I get lonely (I hope he doesn't know that I get scared.) It always seems that whenever I'm lonely, he knows it, and he comes to keep me company. And sometimes he talks to me and tells me things that I don't know, like about the shore house.

It seems as though Laura and Greg have another house that they go to on weekends that is near big water. Moose said it is the biggest water anyone could imagine. It's called the ocean because it's so big. (I'm glad he told me the name, so that if Greg ever says to me that we're going to the ocean, I'll know what he means. Seems like I owe Moose again for that info.)

He tells me that the best part of the house is the deck. A deck is like a patio but this one is up high and you have to look down to see the street. But Moose says that's what's great about it. You can see all of the people on the street, but they can't see you until you bark! He says it's his favorite place in the whole world. The deck. They let him out and he just sits there until someone goes by and then he barks really loudly. And usually he scares the people so much that they stop and watch him barking at them. But the bad thing is that usually when he barks too much Greg will bring him inside until he pretends like he won't bark anymore. Then Greg will let him out on the deck again and it starts all over.

The way Moose makes this shore house sound has me a little worried. First of all, a patio that is way up high? Doesn't anyone realize that maybe a little puppy—a little, tiny, Baby Grady—might not like a deck way up high in the air? Who wants to see people when they can't see you? Isn't the purpose of seeing people to have them see you and tell you what a nice boy you are, and how cute you are, and how big you are? I'll have to wait and see if I like the deck or not.

I asked Moose if we get to go in the car to this other house. He said that we take a ride for about an hour. I don't know how long an hour is, but I know that I like car rides. Car rides are the best! Moose told me that the car ride is great, the house is great, and best of all—the ocean is really close. Greg will take us for walks on the sand and we can play in the water if we want. He says that the kind of boys that we are, we should like water. He says that we are bred to be water rescue boys. And there are great stories about some of our kind—Newfoundlands—saving people stuck in water.

Well, that's all I need to hear. I can't wait to go! I like water—especially nice warm baths when Laura scratches my back. Ocean—here I come!!

The Deck

And that very weekend we do go to the shore house. Moose is right about the car ride. What a great car ride. I guess Laura loves having me ride in the front seat with her because she keeps talking to me and telling me nice things like she always does. And she is watching out for me when Greg turns really fast. I like it when she watches out for me. But we're getting a little cramped, both of us in the same seat. I wonder what they will do when I start getting as big as Moose. Where will Laura sit then?

And now we're here! I can smell the ocean and hear the gulls and feel the wind. Moose didn't tell me how much cooler it would be, but it does feel good. I just put my nose up in the air and let the wind blow through my hair. And I sniff all around so that I'll recognize this place if I ever get lost— you never can be too careful.

We all go through a gate to the back yard—okay, no grass or mud, just all stones. I can deal with that. I can push stones all around and maybe find some mud underneath.

Moose is out back with us and he starts to pee, so I pee too. I guess this is where we go here. I'll play it safe and do whatever Moose does. He knows the ropes here, I don't yet.

Now we all go inside. Lots of steps to climb, but I like steps. Oh, I like this place. Nice and roomy.

Oh no! I thought that this place would be different. But it's not! Why ruin the shore house with a CAGE? Did they think I wouldn't see it? How could they think that they couldn't trust me here?

I know. I'll just keep to the original plan. I'll do whatever Moose does and they'll have to realize that I'm ready to be without a CAGE. After all, they've known me for over a few months now. I'm only in the CAGE at home when they go out in the car, and at night. And at night I'm in a CAGE upstairs in the bedroom now. With Greg, Laura and Moose. And I don't cry anymore, and I sleep until they wake up. Pretty soon I won't need a CAGE there, so why do I need one here?

Well, like I said, I'll do whatever Moose does. If he drinks water, I drink water. If he goes to the kitchen, I go to the kitchen. That's my plan and I'm sticking to it.

Moose is ready to go out on the deck. Laura says something like, "Here we go again," but I don't know what she means. So Greg lets Moose out on the deck. Moose goes out on the deck, I go out on the deck. That's the plan.

And I start to follow him. But he never, ever, told me how high up this deck actually is. Let's just say that it is really high up! So high up that I can't possibly go out there. You can see the ground below through the wood slats! Who would walk on anything that's see-through? Not me. I'm way too careful to be walking on a see-through surface. And frankly, I'm surprised Moose does it. So I ask him.

"Moose, aren't you afraid to be so high above the

ground? What if the deck falls, or you fall through the cracks between the wood, or fall through the holes in the railing? Aren't you scared? You told me I would love the deck, and I can't even step one foot on it."

"Grady, the deck isn't scary. I've been coming out here for years and never once did anything happen. Sometimes when Laura and Greg have visitors, everyone comes out on the deck. And if everyone is on the deck, that's where I want to be. With everyone. Otherwise I might miss something. Oh yeah, and they always have good food out here when it's hot outside. You don't want to miss that, do you?"

"Well, no, I guess I don't. You do make it sound like a nice place to be. I'll try again—I am a trooper you know."

I'll try to put my right paw down first. Laura's telling me that it's okay, so it must be okay. But I am sooo scared. These boards don't seem as sturdy as Moose thinks. And even without being on the deck I can see the porch under it. Oh, what if it fell? I can't do it, I just can't.

But instead of admitting it to Moose or Laura I just play it cool. I tell Moose that I think the deck should be like the patio at home—you know, a place where he can go to get some peace and quiet, and that he doesn't have to share the deck with me. This way, he'll think I'm being a thoughtful, considerate, caring little brother. And Laura, well, I just pretend that I've been on lots of decks before, and that this one is no different, so I really don't have to go out and see it at all. That's my story with her.

And just when I think that I'm cool with her, I hear her say to Greg, "Honey, I think Baby Grady is afraid to go out on the deck."

I am really hoping that the glass door is thick enough that Moose didn't hear that.

Greg says, "Well, we won't make him go out. We'll take him out later with us. Once he sees how much Moose likes it out there, he'll want to go."

That's what he thinks, but I know differently. No matter who is out there, Moose, the visitors with food, Laura and Greg, no matter who, I am *not* going out on that deck.

The Beach

I do sleep in the CAGE at night but it isn't so bad. Laura and Greg both sleep on the floor right near it and Moose is close by too. Just like at home—one big happy family. They really want me to like this place, but so far I'm not so sure. That deck is scary and there's no mud out back. But Moose keeps telling me how great the beach is. And Greg told me he would take me for a walk on the beach, which is right next to the ocean. So I might like this place yet. I'm a trooper, so I'll try this beach thing.

Today Greg is going to take me for the walk. And Laura and Moose are coming too! I am soooo excited that I bark to get the show on the road. I jump up for my leash and grab it because everyone is taking so long. If they don't hurry, I can walk myself. I might not get far 'cause I don't know where the beach is or what the ocean really looks like, but I can start. And I will if they don't hurry!

Okay, I'll wait. Moose has his leash on and I have my leash on and off we go! Oh, what an adventure! I'm going to the beach. I'm going to see the ocean. Moose said I can swim in the ocean, that boys like us were bred to swim. I can't wait. I like the water—the hose and the bath are still up there on my list of great things to do. Even though I am getting too big for the tub, I still like it!

I try to hurry things along and start to lead, but I don't know where I'm going. Greg says, "Grady's just like you, Laura, he wants to lead but doesn't know where he's going."

"Ha ha ha," Laura says. "You're so funny."

I guess he just meant that I'm like Laura— well, that's not so bad. Even though I want to be more like Greg, and most of all, I want to be like Moose.

Moose tells me that the sand leads to the beach which is all sand and then at the end of the sand is the ocean. He says we're almost there! I can't pull hard enough on my leash to hurry Greg. Every time I pull and try to run faster, he pulls me back and gets control. I hate that.

Okay, I feel sand under my feet. That means we're almost there. Deep down I want to play it cool so that Moose and Laura and Greg think that I've been to the beach plenty of times before they knew me. That's how I want to act, but I'm just so excited. Up, over the dune, and OH MY! I can't fake ever seeing this before! It's the ocean. It's so big. And so blue. And I can feel the wind in my hair, smell the salt in my nose, and hear the roar of the waves! The ocean makes noise. And it moves! As long as I live I don't think I'll ever forget how I feel right now.

And Moose is watching me. "Didn't I tell you it's awesome? Wait until you feel it. You're going to love it. Boys like us were bred to love it."

We all run towards the water. At the edge of the water Moose, Greg and Laura stop. They want to watch me run in. So I run in. Man, it is cold with a capital C. I run right back to

Greg. He pats my head and starts to laugh.

"Go ahead, Grady, go for a swim," he tells me.

Okay, I'll try again. I am a trooper. I run into the waves and this time I last a little longer. About ten seconds. I'm telling you, it's cold. And if a wave hits you, it can knock you over. And it tastes really salty. I thought it would taste like the water in my water bowl or at least be as refreshing as the water in the toilet. But no, it's salty and I don't think I like it. So I run back to Greg.

Now Laura is laughing. She can't even talk she is laughing so hard. Well, I don't want her laughing at me, but I don't want to go back in the ocean either. But if she keeps laughing, well, I'll show her. So I do go back into the ocean, but just up to my ankles. And it's not so bad. If you only go in about two inches the waves don't get you, so you won't get knocked down. And you don't get splashed in the face, so you can't taste the salt. So I think I'll just walk along the very edge, and maybe they won't think it's so funny.

They're walking right beside me but they aren't in the water, they're walking on the sand. Moose isn't in the water, Greg isn't in the water and Laura isn't in the water. So why is it so funny that I don't want to be in the water?

Then I find out the answer to that question. In between Laura laughing I hear her saying things to Greg. "This is our third Newfoundland and the third one that doesn't like the water. Is it us? Do we just pick the odd ones? We like the water more than they do. Wait till my mom hears this."

Ah hah! Their third Newfoundland, and their third that doesn't like the water. That means that Moose doesn't like the water! I look over at him and he's smiling too.

"I never said that I like swimming in the ocean. I said that I like to take walks on the beach. And I did think that maybe you would like all the water. You seem to like your baths so much and all."

Well, as long as I know Laura wasn't laughing at me because I was the only weird one. And I like walking on the beach too! I like how the wind blows my hair. And I like Greg hanging around with us and not going to work. We're all walking together. Oh yeah, I like walking on the beach too. And there's nothing funny about that!

The Rescue

For some reason Greg and Laura refuse to admit that I'm not crazy about the ocean. They think that it must be the waves that I don't like, so they are devising a plan to take me to a place that doesn't have waves. It's called the inlet.

Why can't they just understand that it's the whole idea of the ocean that I don't like. I don't like how cold the water is, I don't like the salty taste, and they're right about the waves, I just don't like them. And there are other people on the beach. Any one of which might hurt us at any time. So I have to be on the watch for strangers that might try to hurt Laura or Greg or Moose. I think Moose could handle himself, but I'd have to help. So a day at the beach is really no picnic for me. Too much going on.

Anyway, today we are going to the inlet so I can swim in the ocean without any waves. And the worst thing is that Moose isn't going. Who's going to tell me stuff that I don't know? What if I have questions about this so-called inlet? Oh, why do they think I'll like it anyway?

The ride in the car is kinda different. I get to sit in the back seat all by myself. But I have to ride going sideways. I don't know if I like this. But it is roomy back here. Man, Moose has it made, always riding back here by himself. I do sort of miss

Laura talking to me and petting my ears though. Maybe Moose isn't so lucky.

We park the car and now we have to walk to the inlet. Up and over some dunes—another word for sand that's hard to walk up and over. Oh, now I get it. It's the ocean, but they're right—no waves. This might be okay after all. And Laura and Greg have their bathing suits on, so I think they might get into the water with me! This might be fun yet!

Laura goes in first. "It's pretty cold, but it feels good. Watch the rocks and make sure Baby Grady gets down okay."

"I will, you just be ready to get him when he goes in," yells Greg.

So Greg and I get over the rocks and go to join Laura in the inlet. Greg goes in first, holding onto me with my leash. But hey, since they're both in, and nothing bad is happening, I think I'll try this inlet thing.

Wow! I am all wet, just like in the tub. The water is colder, but I can walk around and the water only comes up to my neck, so I'm okay. Not too scary. And it is pretty nice being here with Greg and Laura all by myself. They're only paying attention to me. And you should hear the encouragement!

"What a big boy, walking in the water all by yourself" and "Baby Grady, what a good swimmer you are, we knew you would like the water." I'm feeling pretty pleased with myself and the whole experience.

But then it happens. Why can't people just leave well enough alone? Greg wants me to come out farther into the water. It looks pretty deep, but he's walking around and he seems okay. What the heck, I'll try it—I'm a trooper and how hard can it be to swim? Millions of people swim every day. And it's not called the doggie paddle for nothing—I mean, we invented it! And I was bred to be a water dog!

So I start to swim over to Greg and Laura. I'm paddling away. I see Laura swim under water so that's how I'm going to swim too. I put my head under and I just keep paddling. Paddling and paddling. Uh oh! I can't breathe! I'm not kidding, I really can't breathe! I was bred to swim and I can't 'cause I can't breathe. What a way to go! I can see people laughing now. The water dog drowns. I can't get a breath, I can't breathe! Someone help me!!

And right then, when I see my much-too-brief life passing before my eyes, Laura puts her hand under my chin and lifts it up out of the water. I can breathe! I can breathe! She saved me!

If I thought I loved her before, let me tell you, I love her a whole lot more now. She's holding me and telling me that it's okay and everything is okay. She's walking in the water with me while I paddle back to shore. She's watching to make sure my head doesn't go under again. And she's still telling me what a good boy I am and what a good swimmer I am and what a trooper I am for even trying to swim in the ocean.

I guess it's okay. I did swim around in the ocean, even if it was just the inlet. I bet Moose never swam in any kind of ocean. She's right, I am a trooper. And I did it. I don't know if I want to do it again, it was pretty scary when I couldn't breathe. No, I don't think I'll do it again, even if they really want me to. I'll just act like once is enough—been there, done that. I would rather try new adventures, if that's okay with you.

Those are the thoughts I'm having as we're driving back to the house. Me in the back seat by myself, being a big guy. Then I see Laura and Greg looking at each other and they start to laugh. Not really loud laughs, but quiet laughs. I didn't hear anyone say anything funny, so I'm at a loss. Then I hear Greg say, "Wait until your mom hears about you saving Baby Grady."

"Shhh, he might hear you," Laura says. "You'll hurt his little tiny baby feelings. It's okay, baby, you swam in the ocean and there aren't a lot of little tiny guys like you that can say that. You're getting to be such a big boy now. Maybe one day we'll try again, but if you don't like to swim in the ocean, that's all right. Moose doesn't like it either and he's a really big guy. Maybe we'll just take walks together—you'll like that."

See, that's why I like Laura. She worries about my feelings and stuff. And she's right about a couple of things—it's okay if I don't like to swim, *and* I do like it when we all take a walk together.

Greg asks Laura, "Why do you treat him like such a baby? You never treated Shadow or Moose like that. He's going to grow up to be a really big dog but act like a puppy if you keep it up."

"I treat him like a baby because he is a baby. He's not like Shadow or Moose, he's just little, tiny, Baby Grady." She's always sticking up for me.

I am still pretty little, not nearly as big as Moose. But I know I'm growing 'cause my CAGE feels smaller to me. And I don't think I act like a baby. Just because I don't like to swim doesn't mean anything. And when we get home I'm going to tell Moose all about swimming in the ocean. I won't mention the rescue part and he'll think I'm pretty big. Yeah, a pretty big guy. Not a baby at all.

And that's just what I tell him. We walk in the door and I run up the stairs to see Moose. "Hey Moose, guess what I did? I swam in the ocean with Laura and Greg. Pretty far out too. Yeah, got a pretty good workout for the first time being in the inlet. I didn't see any other dogs there either. Just me. Guess I'm getting to be a big guy after all. Hey, did you ever swim with them in the inlet?"

"We went to the inlet once, but I didn't want to go in. Greg tried pulling me on my leash, but I refused to budge. So they said, 'Let's not make him,' and we came back home. So I give you a lot of credit, Grady. They couldn't make me swim, and you did it and even liked it. You should be pretty proud of yourself."

Well, actually I don't feel very proud. I feel bad about lying to Moose. He told me the truth and I lied. Oh well, he did say he gives me credit. And I'll take credit from Moose any way I can get it. I did swim in the ocean (I just didn't like it—that's the only lie part). And Moose thinks I should feel proud about it, and so I will feel proud about it.

Houses

We only go to the shore house on some days. Moose calls it the weekend. He loves the shore house. I call those days the me-end. I hate the shore house. There are just too many scary things going on there. There's the deck—I won't go near it. The ocean—I won't go in it. And when you go out back to take care of business, there are a whole lot of people that can see you. No privacy. No privacy whatsoever.

And there seems like there are always people in the house. Our house. We don't have people in the other house. But here, there are always people. And Laura and Greg aren't at home as much. They go out, especially around dinner time, with these people. Don't get me wrong. Most of the people are okay. Some even spend time petting me and saying nice things to me. Some even tell me what a lucky boy I am to have a house at the shore. If they only knew how unlucky I felt.

But I think some are afraid of me. Not because I'm mean, 'cause I'm not, but just because I'm big. I'm still not as big as Moose, so why aren't they afraid of him? He just sits there and hangs out with these people. Like he's known them all his life. Well, maybe he has known them. I haven't known them as long, so naturally I have to sniff and smell them. Even though Laura and Greg seem to know them, you never can be too careful. So I sniff and smell. You know, to make sure they're okay.

Most of these people don't like it when I sniff. Especially the ladies. They always push my head away. And then they walk away. So I just sniff someone else. I am just trying to make sure everyone is safe to have in the house. Laura, Greg, and Moose seem so trusting. Someone has to be careful, and I guess it's up to me.

But, like I said, we aren't always at the shore house. Actually, most of the time we aren't. I don't understand why we ever go—the other house is so much nicer. First of all, it's way more quiet. And there aren't all of these strange people always stopping by to visit and take Laura and Greg places. And there's no deck. And when you go out back to do your business, there's no one that can see you. That's the best part, and why I love it at home. Our "regular" home. Not the shore house. That'll never be my home. But I do have to admit, Moose loves it. I guess it's his other "regular" home. Not mine. Never mine.

Walks

At our "regular" house, almost every night we take walks. I kind of have mixed feelings about walks. In some ways I love them. Greg walks me and Laura walks Moose. That's the part I love. We're all together. I can listen to Greg and Laura talk and find out what they're thinking. And I can talk to Moose and he tells me about the neighborhood and where the best smells are to be found.

But, in some ways I don't like the walks. There are a lot of houses, and a lot of houses means a lot of people. And frankly, people can scare me. They can make loud noises, like closing front doors, or car doors, or just yelling to each other. And each time I hear a loud noise, I jump. I don't know what it is. It could be something that would hurt us. So I always have to be on guard when we walk. Like I said, mixed feelings.

Greg, Laura, and Moose seem pretty comfortable on these walks. Seems like they've done it a lot. Sometimes it's hard for me to imagine that they did it before I came here. I wish I had been born sooner so that I could have always walked with them. And then maybe I would feel comfortable too.

Greg seems to get a kick out of the fact that things scare me. When we're walking he'll say things like, "Look out,

Laura, it's trash night and you know that can be kind of scary." And then they both watch as I'm cautious around the trash. I mean, it's other people's trash! Anything in there could hurt us! Someone has to watch out! Moose doesn't watch out, he just walks with Laura as if trash couldn't hurt any of us. Laura watches me to make sure I'm okay. I think she knows. Even though I'm with Greg, and he's a big guy that could protect us, she needs to know that I'm okay. And when she knows I'm okay, she laughs with Greg. Come to think of it, they both get a kick when something frightens me.

Sometimes Moose doesn't feel like going for a walk. I guess he's getting older and the walks aren't as fun for him anymore. He told me once why sometimes he goes, and sometimes he doesn't.

"When I go for a walk, it's because I really want to go. I love having Laura talk to me on our walks and I love showing you around the neighborhood. And we all get a kick out of watching you get scared at any old shadow or noise. But sometimes my bones hurt too much. I have what the doctor calls 'arthritis.' And I'll tell you, Grady, it's no fun. Sometimes I'm okay, and sometimes I hurt. On the days I hurt, I don't go for a walk. And they don't make me. They know I would if I could."

I didn't know Moose had "arthritis." I hope I never get it. Imagine not being able to go for a walk even if you wanted to go.

When Moose doesn't want to go for a walk, I don't want to go either. I really only like it when we are all together. I can hear what Laura says to Moose, what she says to Greg, what he says to her, what he says to Moose, and what they all say to me! It's just too great! But when Moose doesn't feel up to it, then Laura wants to stay back with him. And even though I like walking with Greg (sometimes I have to admit, I like it just fine. I like the individual attention. He doesn't have to listen to Laura or Moose. Just me.), it isn't the same. I like it best when everyone is there.

So when Moose doesn't feel like going, I don't either. But they make me go. They don't make him go, but they make me go. I try to fight it, and I have a few good tactics, if I do say so myself.

My main one is to hide. I run to the coffee table and go under it. I put my whole body under it. But somehow, Greg always finds me. And Laura laughs.

Another good one is to run upstairs and into the bathroom. Then I just make myself as heavy as possible. That means that when they try and get me, I don't budge. Not an inch. Not even when Laura tries to sweet-talk me. And sometimes this one works. Greg says, "Forget it, he doesn't want to go, I'm not going to force him." So we don't go.

And sometimes it doesn't work. He says, "No way, Grady. You're not winning this time. You need a walk and you're going." And then he picks my rear end up and makes me go. I still try to fight it—it doesn't really hurt, but I make crying noises so that he will think that it hurts me—but most of the time he wins.

And other times, they just plain lie to me. Laura will say that she's going for the walk too. And I never know if it's a time that she's lying or a time that she'll come with us. Because even when Moose doesn't feel like going, sometimes Laura doesn't stay home with him, she comes with us. And sometimes she says she's coming, and she doesn't. I never can tell.

So when I'm pulling the old I-don't-want-to-go-and-you-can't-make-me routine, she'll say things like "I'm coming too, Baby Grady. Let's go for a walk, we'll have such a good time, just the three of us. We all need to get out of the house. Let's go!" So I buy it. I let Greg put the leash on me, all three of us walk to the door, Greg and I go out, and Laura doesn't!!

And I hate to admit it, but I fall for this charade every time. Laura can be so devious!

And so I go for a walk with just Greg. And even though I put up a fight, like I said, I do kind of like it.

Dinner Time

I know I mentioned that Greg and Laura go out sometimes. Usually around dinner time. Sometimes they feed us before they go, sometimes after they come back. I like it when they feed us before they leave. Otherwise, I get sooo hungry. And I complain to Moose. Where are they? When will they be home? Did they forget that we haven't eaten? Don't they know I'm hungry? It's late! When will they be home? What if they don't come home? Oh, I can't even think about that! What would we do? Who would feed us? Oh, where are they?

And Moose always says the same thing, in that deep, comforting voice. "Grades, they always come home for us. They always feed us, and talk to us, and let us out to do our business. As long as I've known them, they've always come home. Sometimes it might take them longer. I remember one time a few years ago, they left for work early in the morning, like any other day. And then there was a big storm, and it took them until almost midnight to get home. And I was by myself. Alone for over fifteen hours. And as you can see, I survived. I had to hold "it" a very long time. Because I won't pee or poop in the house—ever. So I held it. And I got hungry. Very hungry. And I was worried. Like you worry. But the one thing I knew is that they would come and take care of me.

Somehow, I just knew. So this is what you have to remember, they always come home. They always come home."

Well, after listening to Moose's story about waiting until midnight to be let out and waiting until then for dinner, I didn't feel so bad. Moose doesn't talk to me as much as I wish he would, but when he does, I know I should listen. He is pretty smart, and he is pretty old—he's like six or something. And he has been here with Laura and Greg longer than I've been, so I listen. And he makes me feel better. I know if he says they'll come home, they'll come home.

But what if they don't?

Not such a Baby Anymore!

Well, the day has finally come!! Greg and Laura are going out and I'm not going to be in the CAGE! I heard them talking before, and I owe it all to Greg. I knew he was on my side. Laura does kinda treat me like a baby. Greg knows that I'm old enough, and smart enough, and good enough, to be left outside of the CAGE in the house when they aren't here. He knows.

So they're going out and I'm going to be able to go wherever I want. Just like Moose. Wait until he hears this! Just the two of us, hanging out, shooting the breeze, just like I always imagined. I can't wait! What will I do first? Where will I go? Oh, I can't wait!

Then I hear her. Laura, usually my biggest supporter, trying to talk Greg out of it! "I know we'll only be gone an hour or so, but what if he starts chewing? Remember the carpeting with Shadow? Remember the wall? I just don't know."

"I'm telling you, you're treating him like a baby. I think he's ready. And he really is getting too big for the crates. Have you noticed that his head droops when he's inside? That's because he's too big. And those are the biggest crates you can buy. So if he's outgrown them, he should be old

54

enough to be left outside when we go out. And it's only for an hour or so. It won't be long."

Greg makes a good argument. Let's wait and see if she buys it. Please, please. I won't be like Shadow. I don't even know what "chew" means!

"Okay, we'll see how it goes. But if it's a mess when we get home, I call 'no clean-up.'"

Okay, she went for it!

I'm on my own at last! I know Moose is still here, but he's not my boss. I can go anywhere and do anything I want! They're gone, and I'm not in a CAGE!

What do I do? Why does Moose just sit around when he can do anything and go anywhere? I asked him once when I was still in the CAGE, not old enough to be trusted, like I am now. This is what he said:

"I don't run around the house and go everywhere and go wild because there is no reason to do it. Remember, I came here when I was older, and I just wanted Greg and Laura to like me so they wouldn't treat me like my old owners. So I had to be on my best behavior. They had to like me. I really liked them and I didn't want to be sent back to the doctor's where they were going to kill me. Yeah, kill me 'cause nobody wanted a really big dog. So I had to be good. When they left the house, I stayed in one spot. I stayed in the same spot I was in when they left, because I wanted them to know that they could leave and I would be fine.

"To tell the truth, I wasn't fine. Every minute they were gone I missed them. I would just sit and wait until they came home. I missed them so much. And I got scared sometimes, just like you do, but I couldn't let it show. Because I thought that if I acted scared or did anything that was wrong, then they wouldn't like me. And I wouldn't be able to live here anymore. So I had to be extra careful and extra good. I'm telling you, Grady, this is the best place to live. So act up if you want to, but be careful, they can always send you back."

So, that was the answer I got from Moose when I asked. And that's why he just hangs around whether they're here or not. Well, I can't act that way. Especially not my very first time left out of the CAGE. I have to explore. I have to see things, go places, meet people! Well, maybe not meet people—I don't like most, except Laura and Greg.

Okay, they're gone. I'm on my own. Yes sir, I'm old enough to be trusted. Every time I say something like this Moose just looks at me and shakes his head. "Watch out, just watch out," he says. Oh, I'm watching out all right.

Timing is Everything

Right now I'm watching the stairs as I climb them and nobody is home up here. I'm watching as I go into the bedroom and nobody is here either. I'm watching as I go into Greg's office and no one is here! Oh, I could have so much fun in his office! Answer the phone, talk to people, and just like Greg, I could be important. If I told people to do things, they would do them. Yeah, if it weren't so late, I could do some business.

But it is late. Where's my dinner? I like being out of the CAGE and all, but where's my dinner? So instead of hanging around in the office, I go back downstairs. Moose is waiting. I ask him how long an hour is so that I'll know when they will be home. I know I was all excited to be on my own, but I do already miss them. Especially since I'm on my own.

Moose answers my question with, "An hour is as long as it takes them to go to church and back. An hour is as long as one TV show is on before they have other people come on. An hour is as long as it takes them to get ready to go to work in the morning. Okay? Now do you know how long an hour is?"

"Well, yeah I guess. It's kinda long, but not too long. It's the kind of time when you just get used to them being gone, and then they're home again. Yeah, I know how long an hour is. They said they would only be gone an hour, so where are they? Where are they, Moose?"

"It hasn't been an hour yet, Grady. It's only been about ten minutes. I know it seems long because you're out of your crate for the first time and you're all excited, but it really hasn't been long at all."

"Well, why didn't they feed us before they left? What if something happens to them and they can't feed us tonight? What then? I'll tell you what, I'm not waiting. No way am I going to starve to death while they're out having a grand old time. No siree. Not me. I'll fend for myself. I'll find food somewhere in here, or I'll die trying."

"Would you please stop being a drama king? They'll be back soon. I know you don't understand time, but it won't be long. I promise. I wouldn't lie to you, Grady. Even though I wasn't so thrilled about you coming to live with us, you've grown on me. I like you. And I'm telling you to settle down. They will be home. They always come home."

Well, those were certainly nice words and all, and Moose has the nicest voice I've ever heard, and I don't know what I would do if Moose weren't here to talk to me, but where's my food? I know where they keep it. I'll just get it myself, thank you very much.

A Hunter or a Gatherer?

Okay, I can get in this door. It's not the big bag of food that they usually use, but it's the one they use to take food to the shore house. We aren't going to the shore house, but it's still filled with kibble. Oh, I love kibble. And I am sooo hungry. Uh-oh, it's stuck. They must have it on a special hook or something. I don't care, I'll get it one way or another. Pull, pull, tug, tug, pull. Oh, I'll get it all right.

"Got it! Got it! Moose, look! Food! Wonderful, glorious, free food!! I'll just dump the bag on the kitchen floor and we can both eat. I'm pretty good at sharing, I think. C'mon Moose! Come and get the food that I found! It's all over the kitchen floor—just come and get it! Oh, if I had never been in a CAGE we could have had this all the time. I'm a pretty good food getter, if I do say so myself. Look at it—just look at it! It's all over the place. Who could ask for more? I knew they should have let me out of the CAGE sooner. I knew I was ready!"

Moose says that we're going to get in trouble. I don't believe it. "Why? Why would we get in trouble for trying to feed ourselves when Greg and Laura aren't here? Who else would feed us if I don't? No one, that's who. It's up to me. And look, I did it!"

"You should have just waited, Grady. First of all, we don't need this much food. We couldn't eat this much food in a week! Look, it's all over the kitchen floor. We can't even walk on the floor, there's so much food on it. And second, I think Laura will get mad. She always tries to keep this floor clean. She spends a lot of time washing and waxing it. Yeah, I hate to say it to you on your first day out of the crate, but I think she's going to get mad. And remember, she wasn't that thrilled with you being out of the crate tonight. You didn't have to do this, I'm telling you, they come home. And they feed us. Always."

"Well, you can play it safe, but I'm going to eat! I don't think they give us enough food to begin with. So finally, I get us enough food and you don't want it. That's okay. I'll eat it all. Or at least I'll eat until I can't anymore. Look! It's fun! Eat, eat, eat. Oh, I like food all right. Yeah, I like food. I wish we had some of the wet food, but I'm happy with all of this dry stuff. More food than I ever imagined! Oh, I love food! Come on, Moose, they might not be home for a while! Eat up!!"

At last Moose does come into the kitchen to eat. But he only eats as much as he normally would have eaten. And he keeps saying that we will get in trouble. But I know he thinks it is fun, even if he won't admit it.

And it was fun. I ate so much that I thought I would burst. And then we sat in the living room and laughed. Just laughed. Just me and Moose. Two brothers. Laughing about the food I found and the food we ate, and the food Laura's not going to like to see on the kitchen floor. There's still a lot of food out there. I can't take another bite, but there is still a lot of food out there.

Maybe Moose is right. Maybe Laura will be mad. I really don't want that to happen, but I can't possibly eat all of the food left on the floor. It's like a whole week's worth!

"Pretty soon they'll be home. Well, maybe they'll be mad, maybe they won't. I still have time left and I'm not in my CAGE, so I'll still try to have a good time. You with me Moose?"

"No, but you go ahead. Have fun. I'll tell you one thing I've learned, you might as well do everything bad that you want to do. You can only get in so much trouble. They might yell and smack your nose, but they do that if it's a little bit of trouble or a whole lot of trouble. So, since you're already going to be in trouble, you might as well have more fun."

Birds of a Feather

So I go upstairs and jump on the bed. Oh, I love being on the bed. There is a mirror straight across and I can watch myself. If I lean my head to the left, the mirror shows it. If I stick out my tongue, the mirror shows it. If I nod up and down, the mirror does too. Yeah, I love looking at myself. People are right about one thing—I'm gorgeous. I'm so pretty, cute, precious, beautiful, and gorgeous. Just like they say. Yeah, I like looking at myself.

And I just like being on the bed. I mean, this is where Laura and Greg usually are, so it smells like them. So even though they aren't here right now, I can still smell them and it makes me feel better. I can smell a pillow. Oh, it smells just like Laura. I love that smell. I can almost hear her talking to me and petting me just by smelling that smell.

The pillow. I never ate a pillow before. Even though I'm not hungry right now, this minute, 'cause I just ate like a week's worth of food, I think I'll try the pillow. It sure does smell good. It must be good to taste. Imagine tasting a pillow that smells so good. Why imagine? I'll do it.

Rip, rip. Tear, tear. Oh, I'm there. Inside the pillow. What? What's this? Feathers? That's all that's here? Feathers? Just like the ones on birds?

Well, I'm really not looking forward to eating feathers, so I'll just keep looking. There has to be something better to eat inside this pillow. After all, Laura likes to sleep on it, so it must be good. But all I'm finding are feathers. Feathers, feathers. They sure are small. There must be a million of them, and not one that I feel like eating. I'll just keep looking. It seems like I might get somewhere if I swing my head back and forth and get the feathers to fly around. Away from me. I don't like them all around me, so I'll swing them farther away. That's it. On Laura's dresser and Greg's dresser and all on the floor. Away from me, but I'll still keep looking. There has to be something besides feathers in this pillow. But all I'm finding are feathers. Feathers and more feathers. I think we're past a million now—probably up to a gazillion. A gazillion feathers and nothing good to eat in the whole pillow.

But before I can keep looking, I hear Laura and Greg open the front door. Uh oh, where do I go? Where can I hide? The food is still on the floor, and there are little tiny feathers all over the bedroom! Moose is right, I'm going to be in trouble! And my first night out of the CAGE! They'll never let me out again! I thought I'd have time to clean it up. I'd clean it all up and let them know that I can be trusted. But no time. I told Moose I didn't know how long an hour was. It sure seemed like they were gone only ten minutes. Isn't that what Moose said? They were only gone ten minutes. But that was awhile ago when he told me that. Oh, I'm doomed!

The first voice I hear is Laura's. Normally so soft and sweet and just saying nice things. It's a different story now. She walks in the house and sees Moose. "Moose, where is he? Grady, get down here." But I can't. I never had Laura mad at me before, so I can't move. I'm up on the bed, with feathers all around me, and I can't move. I never had her mad at me before. And I don't like the sound of it.

She comes up the steps. She doesn't exactly take me by surprise—I hear her coming and all. But the look on her face takes me by surprise. Yeah, she's mad. Real mad. She just keeps looking around the room and making funny noises. Like "Agh" and "Oahh," and then she says what I didn't want to hear. "You will not be left out of your crate for a long time now, Baby Grady. You are still too little, whether Greg thinks so or not. And you're going to have to help me clean up these gazillion feathers. You made the mess, you clean it up. That's my motto."

I don't know what to do, I mean, I don't know how to clean up a gazillion feathers. But I don't think Laura knows how to clean them up either. But she keeps me in the bedroom while she runs the vacuum. And she is mad, but not too mad. I know that because every once in a while she'll laugh and say, "Grades, I knew you were just a baby. But I never knew how many feathers were in a feather pillow. Who would know? The pillow's not that big. Who would know that there'd be a gazillion feathers? Not I, Baby Grady, not I."

And just when I was thinking that anyone could misjudge how many feathers were in a feather pillow, and I wasn't in that much trouble, I heard her say the words I dreaded. "Greg, I swear, next time you think he's old enough to be left out of the crate, he's staying in!"

And then I hear Greg yell, "He should be helping me clean up all of the kibble food in the kitchen. It's a mess! And I have Moose looking at me as if to say, 'It really wasn't me—you know I don't do things like this when you're gone.' I hate to say it, but I think you were right. Grady still needs the crate."

Oh no! Oh no! Moose was right, I am in trouble. But I had no idea that it would mean the CAGE again. If I had known that, I would have stayed right in the living room and not gotten into the food or gone upstairs to get into the feather pillow or anything. I would have been good! I really, really, really would have been. And the next time when they go out, I wouldn't have to be put in the CAGE. I'll never do anything like this again. I promise. Just look into my eyes and you'll know I mean it. Never, ever.

Right now I'm so upset I want to cry. Cry like I did when I was a baby. They gave me one chance to be trusted and I blew it. Blew it. 'Cause I didn't listen to Moose, and I was hungry.

I mean, I was hungry. Who knew when they would be home to feed us? In a way, it's their fault. If they had been here, none of this would have happened. Not really my fault at all.

But, like I said, I blew it. Who knows the next time I'll be left out of the CAGE? Maybe not 'til I'm one hundred or something.

But now it's the next day and I don't think they're so mad at me. At breakfast I even heard Laura say to Greg, "Can you imagine what he thought when he found all of that food? He must have thought he died and went to heaven. And it was a pretty heavy bag, he must have been so determined to drag it out. I wonder if Moose ate any of it. Or if he just knew it was something that shouldn't be happening. I wonder. Anyway, I can't stop thinking about how Baby Grady must have felt. Like he found the Holy Grail or something. All the food he wants! Anytime he wants! Oh, Greg, he's so funny. And I don't even want to talk about the pillow."

And then she laughs. If there is one thing I know, it's that if Greg or Laura laugh, then it's not too bad. Actually, I think that's when they like me the most. I make them laugh. I don't think Moose makes them laugh so much. I make them laugh. The food on the kitchen floor, the feathers all over the upstairs, yeah, sooner or later they laugh about it. I make them laugh. That's what I do. So my first night out of the CAGE wasn't all bad. I had fun, no one got hurt, and I made them laugh!

The Next Time

Well, needless to say, the next few times that Laura and Greg go out I'm stuck in the CAGE. Just like before. I am in the CAGE and Moose can go anywhere. "Oh, it's just not fair. Why do I have to be in here?"

"Why do you think I can be left on my own, Grady? Because they can trust me. I've never made a mess or ruined anything since I've been here. And they know that. So they trust me. You've got to earn their trust. You can do it in little pieces. When they're home and you're out of the crate, just be good. Don't make them watch you every minute. Just don't get into anything. Then they'll think that you're old enough and good enough to do that when they aren't here. See?"

"Oh, I get it. When they're here I'll be good, so they'll think I'll be good when they're not here. Okay, now that's a plan. I think it might work."

So now I am a little angel when I'm out in the yard—no more mud baths for me, thank you, I'm too old and too good for that now. And I'm a little angel when I'm in the house too. Look, Laura, I'm just hanging out with Moose, doing what he's doing, (or should I say doing what he's *not* doing—man, he can be such a bore). Look, look. I'm a good boy now. Certainly one that you can trust.

"Moose, old buddy, I think this plan was genius. I can tell they both think that I'm getting older and better. I bet the next time they go out I'll be without the CAGE. I bet!"

"Grady, I didn't mean for you being good to be a 'plan.' It's how you're supposed to act. All the time. Just be nice and people will be nice to you. It's not a plan, it's a way of life."

"Okay, I get it. You want people to like you and you want to be Mr. Nice Guy. Well, I think we just want different things in life, Moose. I don't really care if people like me that much. Most people just plain scare me. All those smells and noises that they make. And besides, they do like me and I haven't been that good. They like me anyway.

"What I want right now is for Greg and Laura to think I'm good so I don't have to be left in the CAGE. That's my goal here, and I just want to say thanks for the plan. I think it's working."

And it does work! Like a charm. Laura sits down next to me on the stairs and tells me that she's going out for dinner and Greg is away, so Moose and I will be on our own. She says that she knows I'm too big for the CAGE and that since I'm such a big boy now that she can give me a chance to be out with Moose. She tells me to act just like I do when I'm out of the CAGE during the day. She tells me to pretend that she is right there with me. And just act like the good boy that I am. Oh, thank you—thank you.

"But I mean it, Baby Grady. No messes. I'll only be gone an hour, so why don't you try and get some rest. Just take a little nap. Or do what Moose does. Just don't get into anything. Or you'll be staying in the crate until you're old and gray," she says. And I think she means it.

Okay, okay, I hear ya. Just hurry up and go. I'll do whatever Moose does (or doesn't do), and I'll be good. You'll see. Just go!

"Man, I never thought she would leave. But here we are, Moose. On our own, no CAGES or anything. What do you want to do? Eat something?"

"I don't want to do anything with you. And I suggest that you don't do anything either. Remember the last time? I know you can be good, and I don't want to see you back in the crate next time. I like having you out with me. Why don't we just hang out together?"

"Sure, I like hanging out. And I like hanging out with you especially. Where should we go? Upstairs? In the living room, family room, kitchen? Just tell me where you want to go, and I'm right there with you."

"Since you got into trouble in the kitchen and bedroom last time, why don't we try the family room? I think it'll be safe for you."

So we go into the family room and Moose sits down in his favorite spot. So I go to my favorite spot and sit. He's right about one thing. It is safe for me in here. Two couches, a couple of tables, a TV, a bookshelf, and plants. Laura does like to have plants in each room. I don't know why, but she does. I mean they really don't serve any purpose. They don't talk or walk. And you can't eat them.

Or can you?

I've never seen Greg or Laura or Moose eat any of the plants, but that doesn't mean I can't try. I've never tried before. Maybe I'll like them. Maybe they can be eaten, it's just that no one ever thought to try before. I'll be the first. I'll take the risk. Maybe eating house plants will become all the rage. Everyone will start doing it, and I'll become famous. A famous discoverer. I like that.

I'll start with the one in front of the window. The really big one. The leaves do look kinda tasty. Here goes nothing! Hey, when I grab it in my mouth, I can move the whole plant! "Look Moose! I can drag the plant, and try eating it all at once! And if I spill it on its side, the dirt can come out. And it's wet dirt - just like mud! Oh, I love mud!

"The plant doesn't taste too hot, but I like feeling this mud on my toes. Makes me think of when I was baby."

"That's because you're acting like a baby now! Do you think Laura wants that plant spilled all over the family room and you tracking mud all over the place? Well, do you?"

"I didn't think of that. I only wanted to taste the plant, and the mud thing, well, it kind of just happened. Don't be mad. I still want to taste some of these other plants.

"To reach the one on the shelf I'll have to climb on the couch, then step on the table. Got it! Oops! I thought I had it, but then it just fell out of my mouth. Now it's all over the floor too. I know, I'll try the one that looks like a tree in the corner."

"I wouldn't if I were you. You know it will mean the crate. Think about that for one minute, will you?"

"Well, I would stop and think about that but I just have to try the tree first. Hey, I can drag this one pretty easily. I bet if I knock it over I can get more mud. I'll try. Nope. Hey, I don't even think this one is real! Moose, a fake plant. Go figure. The leaves don't taste good, but you can take them right off the tree pretty easily. Look how easily they come off! Look! I bet I can get every last one off. Yep, every last one."

"I did learn something here. There is a reason people don't eat houseplants. They don't taste good. How would I have known that unless I tried? Okay, now what?"

"Maybe you should just sit and think about how mad Laura is going to be when she sees this mess. The whole room looks like a backyard after it rains. As a matter of fact, I don't want to have anything to do with this mess. I'm going in the living room."

"Don't worry, Mr. Nice Guy. She'll know you didn't do this. Even if you did do it, she would still think it was me. She'll always think I'm the one that makes the mess!"

"That's probably because you *are* the one that makes the mess."

"Well, no more messes tonight. I'm coming into the living room with you."

Okay, I'll just sit and do nothing. You can't make a mess when you're not doing anything. That much I know. Sit, sit. Nothing, nothing.

Well, all this sitting is for the birds. I need something to eat! But there's no food around, now that they make sure the food closet is always closed. I wonder if anyone ever tried to eat the white couch before. Hmm, I wonder.

Probably not, it doesn't look like anyone ever tried. But that doesn't mean I can't try. I can always try. I know, I'll pull the bottom cushion off the couch and lay on it. While I'm laying on it, I'll quietly nibble. Just a corner at first, then if I like it, who knows? It's a big couch.

Here goes. It's a little harder to pull off than I first thought. Hard, but not impossible. Okay, it's down. And it does feel soft under my belly. Uh oh. I forgot I had mud on me. I don't even have to ask Moose about that one. I know Laura isn't going to like mud on the white couch. Oh well.

Now for the chewing. It does feel good to chew the material—it makes my whole mouth feel good—*but,* it doesn't taste like food. I don't know what it tastes like, but when I pull some of the foam-stuff out of the cushion I can chew on that too. I don't really like the taste at all, but I like to watch it fly in the air and float down. Reminds me of the feathers.

Uh oh. What have I done? I made another mess. Without really thinking about it or trying to do it, I made a mess. I can't even look at Moose. I just don't want to hear it.

Maybe if I try to clean it up. Yeah, I've watched Laura clean enough times. Just get everything into one corner and then throw it away. That's what I'll do. Piece by piece I'll take the parts of the cushion into that corner. It will look much neater then.

I have the fourth or fifth piece in my mouth on the way to the corner to put it in the pile when Laura walks in the front door.

She looks at the mess, puts her back to the wall and slides all the way downs so she is sitting on the floor. She puts her head in her hands and just sits there. So, naturally I want to make her feel better, so I walk over to lick her face. I think she'll like me doing that.

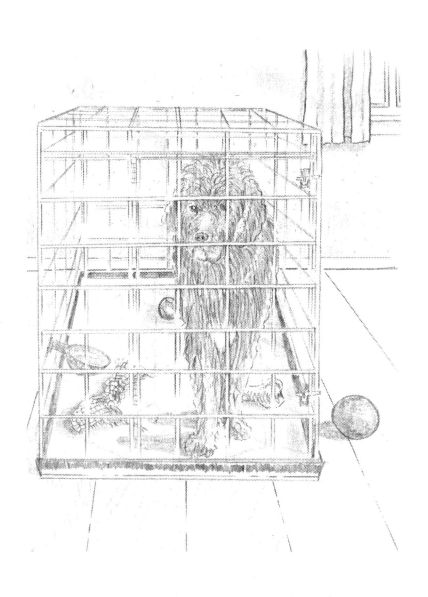

The Best Laid Plans

After the family room plant incident, and the cushion eating episode, I have to stay in the CAGE every time they go out. Greg even bought a bigger CAGE. He says that it's the biggest that they make. Grandma calls it the condo. But I know it's a CAGE.

But when Laura and Greg are home I don't need to be in the CAGE nearly as much as before. And I'm trying to do what Moose told me. When I'm not in the CAGE and they're home, I'm on my very best behavior. Acting more like Moose all of the time. And I'm not doing it as part of a plan, but just doing it. I have to admit, it is easier. I lie around a lot and let them take care of me. I'm definitely on their schedule.

They like to sleep, I like to sleep. So I sleep now until they get up in the morning, sometimes longer. They like to watch TV, I like to watch TV. They like to sit in the kitchen and eat, well, hey, I'm a world class eater. They like to take walks, I like to take walks. Even if Moose doesn't go.

So it's not like I have to do anything special to be good. It's kinda coming naturally to me now. And Moose was right, it should be a way of life, not a plan to get them to let me out of the CAGE. But if me being good does get me out of the CAGE, well, it can be a plan *and* a way of life.

And finally, like after a very long time, the plan does work. I'm going to be left out on my own again when they go out. I heard Laura tell Greg, "Really, Greg, it's getting ridiculous. He's bigger than the condo now. He just looks like he's ready to pop out of the crate. And he's been so good lately. He doesn't eat any plants or go near the couch. We're only going to be gone for about an hour or so, so why not try it?"

And then Greg says, "Well, you were the one that had to clean up the plant and cushion mess. Let's not forget the feathers and food either. So it's up to you. If you say he's ready, then we'll let him out. But I call 'no-clean-up.'"

"I do think he's ready. Let's just try it. He *has* to be ready one of these times."

I told you she's usually my biggest supporter.

And then it happens. Once again, I'm left out of the CAGE while they aren't home. And just like Moose and I discussed, I am going to be good. After all, like I said, it's just not that hard anymore. Actually, it's pretty easy. Watch.

"Hey Moose. Look at me. Being good and all. Just like you told me to be a long time ago. I couldn't do it then, but just watch me now. Just watch me."

Then Moose says the nicest thing to me. In that deep, deep voice he has, he says "You should be very proud of yourself, Grady. You've come a long way. I'm proud of you and I think Greg and Laura will be proud too. They're right. You are ready to be out on your own in the house."

Wow! Moose thinks that I'm great. Maybe he didn't say "great," but he is proud. And he wouldn't be proud if I weren't great. Go figure. Moose proud of me. And I always thought that I could never be as good as Moose. Not anymore. No siree. I'm as good as Moose. I *am* as good as Moose. Maybe better. Sure, better. Maybe the best dog ever. Maybe the best dog the world has ever seen!

"Okay, now what, Moose? What do we do now?"

"We just hang around until they get home, that's what. Have some quiet time, catch up on some sleep. I don't know, just relax and do whatever you want. Except get into trouble. You're too old for that now. There isn't a crate big enough to hold you. And that means that no dog your size, and your age, has ever needed to be put in a crate. Think about that before you do anything foolish."

"Well, I'm not going to do anything foolish. You're right. I am too big to be in a CAGE. I'll never go in that CAGE again. I'll be good, and I'll stay out of the CAGE! Forever!

"So, let's celebrate my first night of freedom! I mean, I know I've been out of the cage before, but let's celebrate the fact that they'll be throwing the CAGES away soon. No more use for them. Obsolete—that means not needed anymore!"

What Should We Do?

"First, you don't know that this is your first night of freedom. They're only gone for an hour. You know that sometimes they go out for longer than that. And they might still put you in a crate then. So settle down. Just relax and appreciate the moment."

"Appreciate the moment? Appreciated the moment, you say? Well, let me tell you something, old pal. I'm appreciating the moment. You have no idea what it's been like being in the CAGE all of these months. No idea. Me in the CAGE, and you just walking around. Going wherever you want to go. Doing whatever you want to do. It's been bad.

"And the worst part is that Greg and Laura always think that you are the 'good' one. I hear them talking to you. I hear her say things like 'You know you're my favorite, Moose. You'll always be my favorite. You're such a "pookie". No one will ever be a "pookie" like you.'

"How do you think that makes me feel? Huh? She thinks I don't hear her, but I do. And she thinks I'm the trouble-maker. Well, I'm not a trouble-maker. I'm just not you!

"And I can never be like you. No matter how hard I try. I just can't.

"And now I don't even feel like celebrating anymore. I never thought I'd say those things to you. I mean, admit that I heard her and all. I know it's not your fault. She likes you best. That's all there is to it. I try to make it sound like it's not that important to me, but even when I say the words, I feel like crying."

Then Moose says the second thing tonight that makes me feel better. He always makes me feel better. Even when I'm mad at him, he tries to make me feel better.

Anyway, he says, "I know what you're thinking, Grady. I know she tells me those things. But you have to remember that Laura and I go way back. I knew her for five years before you came along. And I've tried to be good for five years because I want her to love me. And she does. I know she loves me. But that doesn't mean she doesn't love you. She just says those things to me to make me feel better. So that I don't think she loves you more than me.

"Because to tell you the truth, Grady, when you first came here I was sure that Greg and Laura would like you more. I mean, you're so little and cute. And full of energy. I thought they liked that energy stuff and that I would be forgotten about. So I tried to keep up. Go for walks and stuff. But then I realized something important. When she says those things to me, she does mean it. I know she loves me. They both love me.

"But that doesn't mean that they don't love you. I can see it in their eyes. When he looks at you, when she looks at you. They love you. Believe me, they love you. They wouldn't put up with you if they didn't love you! And they've had a lot to put up with—so they must love you a whole lot. Just remember, they can love both of us. They love me because I've been here longer and I've worked really hard to get them to love me. Remember, my first family didn't love me.

"And they love you because you're so cute. And by the way, I hear what Laura says to you too, you know. I hear her telling you that you are the cutest, funniest, smartest little baby. And she tells you how much she loves you all the time. I hear it. I just know that she loves us both. And you should know it too. She loves us both."

Well, now that he puts it that way, I think I know how they feel about us. They do love us both. And if Laura likes Moose more, like she's always whispering to him, well, I think Greg likes me more. But I won't tell Moose. It might hurt his feelings.

But all of this talk has made me want to do something. I don't know what I feel like doing, but I feel like doing something. Maybe just walk around the house. And visit the old white couch. Oh, I remember how much trouble I got into because of this white couch. To think that I thought I could eat it. Like anyone would eat a couch. Like it even tastes good. If I remember correctly, it doesn't. It doesn't taste good at all. But then, it has been a while. Maybe it tastes different now. If I pull the cushion off the bottom, maybe I'll just see if it tastes as bad as I remember.

"Oh, Grady. Don't do it. They'll be home any minute now. Can't you just wait? You were being so good! Just keep it up and you'll never have to be in the crate again. Think of how proud you'll be when they come home and see that you can be trusted. Just think for a minute. Please."

Well, okay. There, I thought about it for a minute, and I still want to taste the couch. Pull, pull, tug, tug. Much easier to pull it off this time. Now that I'm so big and everything. Much easier. Rip, rip. Tear, tear. Oh, the foam. I remember the foam. It does come out pretty easily. I'm not tasting anything that I can't live without, but what about down deeper? I'll just keep digging and pulling it apart till I get what I want.

I'm done. Just as I remembered. That couch doesn't taste good at all. Why did I think it would? Go figure.

Oh, man. Look what I've done! Oh, no! I can't believe I did it again! It's a mess in here, and I'm to blame. Not that they would ever think it was Moose, but they'll know it's me cause I did it before! How stupid. How absolutely, positively stupid. With a capital S.

Just as I'm supposed to be celebrating my new-found independence, I blow it. Oh, why? Why me? Why am I always getting in trouble?

But before I can even beat myself up anymore over the stupidity and immaturity of the act, in walk Laura and Greg. Not like last time when it was just Laura, this time Greg is with her. And boy he can yell when he feels like yelling. So much for me thinking that he likes me best. No siree, not now. He's not liking me one bit!

"What is wrong with you, Grady? We were gone for an hour! One hour, and you can't be good! What were you thinking? That we wouldn't see this mess? That we wouldn't notice our couch was eaten? You ate our couch! Laura, who eats a couch?"

"No one I know. Oh, I take that back. I do know someone who eats a couch. I'll tell you who eats a couch.

Grady. Baby Grady eats couches, Greg. Little, tiny Baby Grady is now big enough to eat a couch. Go figure.

"But seriously, Greg, what are we going to do? He doesn't fit in that huge crate, and we were only gone for an hour. We have to be able to go out. What are we going to do? And look at that couch. And we can't even think about getting a new one until he stops with this. Look at the mess!"

Uh, oh. She sounds mad. Not as mad as the first time, but kinda mad. And I don't need Moose to tell me that she's disappointed. I can see it in her eyes.

Well, what can I do? I'm not going to go over there so she can pet me. She probably doesn't feel like petting me right now. I know, I'll just keep a low profile for a few days.

Low Profile Days

The low profile plan seemed to work. By the time they were to go out again, I didn't go in my CAGE. But it wasn't because they trusted me. They don't. They'll never trust me like they trust Moose.

The truth is that they just don't care about the couch anymore. I heard Laura this morning say, "We can't keep putting him in a crate—he's just too big. And he has to get bored. He doesn't exactly get thrilled over a chew toy anymore. Let's leave him out. He's so good with us when we're home. He's such a cuddler and a nice boy to be around. I think he just misses us and wants us to know it. You know, negative attention is still attention, and all that psychology stuff. I think that's why he acts up. He just misses us.

"And if he eats the couch, he eats the couch. We need to get a new one now anyway. And it *is* the only bad thing he does now."

And I also heard Greg. "Well, I leave it up to you again. You're right about the couch—no fixing it now. But I just don't understand why he pulls it apart, anyway. Why does he do that? He doesn't eat it, he just pulls it apart!"

"I have no idea. Who ever knows what Baby Grady is

thinking. Sometimes I think I know, and then he does something so off the wall that I'm even surprised. He's just so funny. He doesn't think like normal people. He has his own little agenda, and he sticks to it. You know how stubborn he can be. He's like a grandpa in some ways, and a puppy in a whole lot of ways. I don't understand him, I just like him. He cracks me up. He's a definite keeper. I'd rather have him than a couch anyday."

Well, I'm a keeper. To think that I might not have been at this late stage of the game! I've been here for over a year, and she just now decides to keep me? Oh, maybe she was kidding. I'm sure she was. They were going to keep me all along. Just because I chew the couch doesn't mean they would get rid of me! No siree, they need a new couch anyway. I heard them.

I'm part of the family now. Me, Greg, Laura, and Moose. What a great family. Moose said he had to work to get them to love him. I think they fell in love with me naturally. But from now on, I am going to work to make sure they stay in love with me. I really want to be a keeper. And I want to be kept right here. Forever and always. Me, Greg, Laura, and Moose. Together forever.

And when I think about that, I don't even feel like chewing a couch.

Maybe I'm not a baby anymore.

Printed in the United States
20634LVS00006B/490